Cats Everywhere

by Patricia Gangas
illustrated by Bruce MacDonald

Richard C. Owen Publishers, Inc.
Katonah, New York

I see cats on the table,

cats on the floor,

cats on the bed,

cats by the door.

I see cats in the garden,

cats in the shed,

cats at the window,

cats on the ledge.

Everywhere, everywhere, cats fill the house.

What a wonderful place,

if I weren't a mouse!